The Pout-Pout Fish Cleans Up the Ocean

Deborah Diesen

Pictures by **Dan Hanna**

Farrar Straus Giroux
New York

*For Dan Hanna, who brings the beauty and wonder of the ocean
to life on the page —D.D.*

*For Deborah Diesen, whose heart is as wide and deep as the ocean,
and for those who work and fight for the health of our planet —D.H.*

Farrar Straus Giroux Books for Young Readers
An imprint of Macmillan Publishing Group, LLC
175 Fifth Avenue, New York, NY 10010

Text copyright © 2019 by Deborah Diesen
Pictures copyright © 2019 by Dan Hanna
All rights reserved
Color separations by Embassy Graphics
Printed in China by RR Donnelley Asia Printing Solutions Ltd.,
Dongguan City, Guangdong Province
Designed by Aram Kim
First edition, 2019
10 9 8 7 6 5 4 3 2 1

mackids.com

Library of Congress Cataloging-in-Publication Data

Names: Diesen, Deborah, author. | Hanna, Dan, illustrator.
Title: The pout-pout fish cleans up the ocean / Deborah Diesen ; pictures by Dan Hanna.
Description: First edition. | New York : Farrar Straus Giroux, 2019. |
   Summary: Mr. Fish and an increasing number of sea creatures investigate, then decide how to deal with,
   a huge mess in the ocean. Includes tips for the reader to help clean up and protect the ocean.
Identifiers: LCCN 2018039309 | ISBN 9780374309343 (hardcover)
Subjects: | CYAC: Marine pollution—Fiction. | Pollution—Fiction. |
Ocean—Fiction. | Marine animals—Fiction. | Environmental protection—Fiction.
   Classification: LCC PZ8.3.D565 Pom 2019 | DDC [E]—dc23
   LC record available at https://lccn.loc.gov/2018039309

Our books may be purchased in bulk for promotional, educational,
or business use. Please contact your local bookseller or the Macmillan
Corporate and Premium Sales Department at (800) 221-7945 ext. 5442 or
by email at MacmillanSpecialMarkets@macmillan.com.

"The ocean is amazing!"
Mr. Fish's grin was wide.
The beautiful surroundings
Left him wonderstruck inside.

His head was full of happy
And his heart was full of awe,

But his smile sank away
When he turned around and saw . . .

A big . . .

BIG . . .

MESS!

"Whatever could it be?"
But he couldn't really tell.
So he talked with a friend
Who had noticed it as well.

"There's a problem that needs solving,
And I don't know what to do.
But I'm going to find some answers.
Would you like to join me, too?"

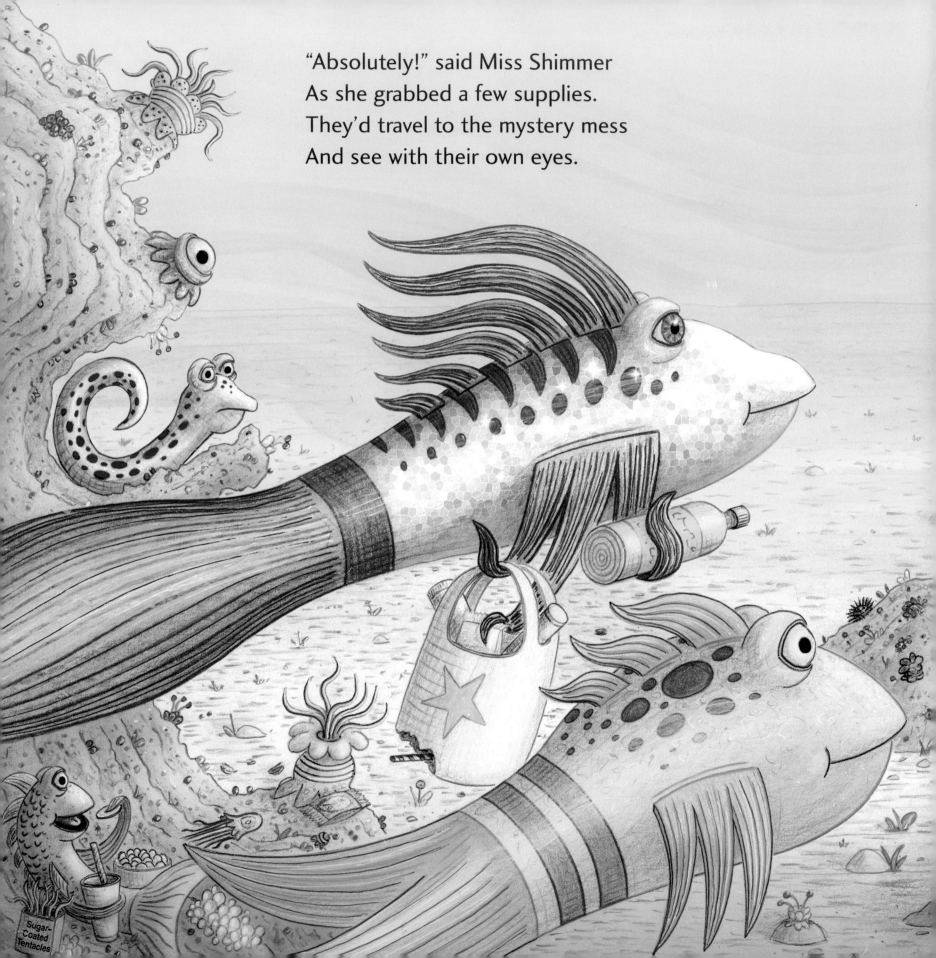

"Absolutely!" said Miss Shimmer
As she grabbed a few supplies.
They'd travel to the mystery mess
And see with their own eyes.

Swimming off, they were enchanted
By the ocean big and bright.
But looming in the distance
Was that dark, dismal sight:

A big . . .

BIG . . .

MESS!

"What's it made of?" they both wondered,
And they pondered this out loud.
Around them, others gathered
In a small but growing crowd.

"There's a problem that needs solving,
And we don't know what to do.
But we're going to find some answers.
Would you like to join us, too?"

"Count us in!" said Mr. Seahorse,
And he powered up his rig.
Enthusiasm bubbled—
Yes, the group was getting big!

They jetted through the ocean
In a peaceful sort of bliss,
But the thing that stretched before them
Was impossible to miss:

"Who will fix it?" fish were asking,
Hoping someone else would know.
There was lots of conversation
As they traveled with the flow.

"There's a problem that needs solving,
And we don't know what to do.
But we're going to find some answers.
Would you like to join us, too?"

SAM'S
Tacos,
Donuts &
Wedding
Cakes

"All as one!" said Mrs. Squid
As she swished away some junk.
The group continued forward
Toward the nearing pile of gunk.

They reached the mystery mess.
They took measurements and samples.
They made notes, and they did research.
They found similar examples.

When everyone was finished,
They assembled to discuss.
They came to one conclusion:

"The problem is . . .

They froze in disbelief,
Then they all began to shout,
Feeling troubled and uneasy.
And some began to pout!

Were they stuck with this forever?
Would it worsen? Would it grow?
Mr. Fish was worried, too—
"But there's one thing that I know . . .

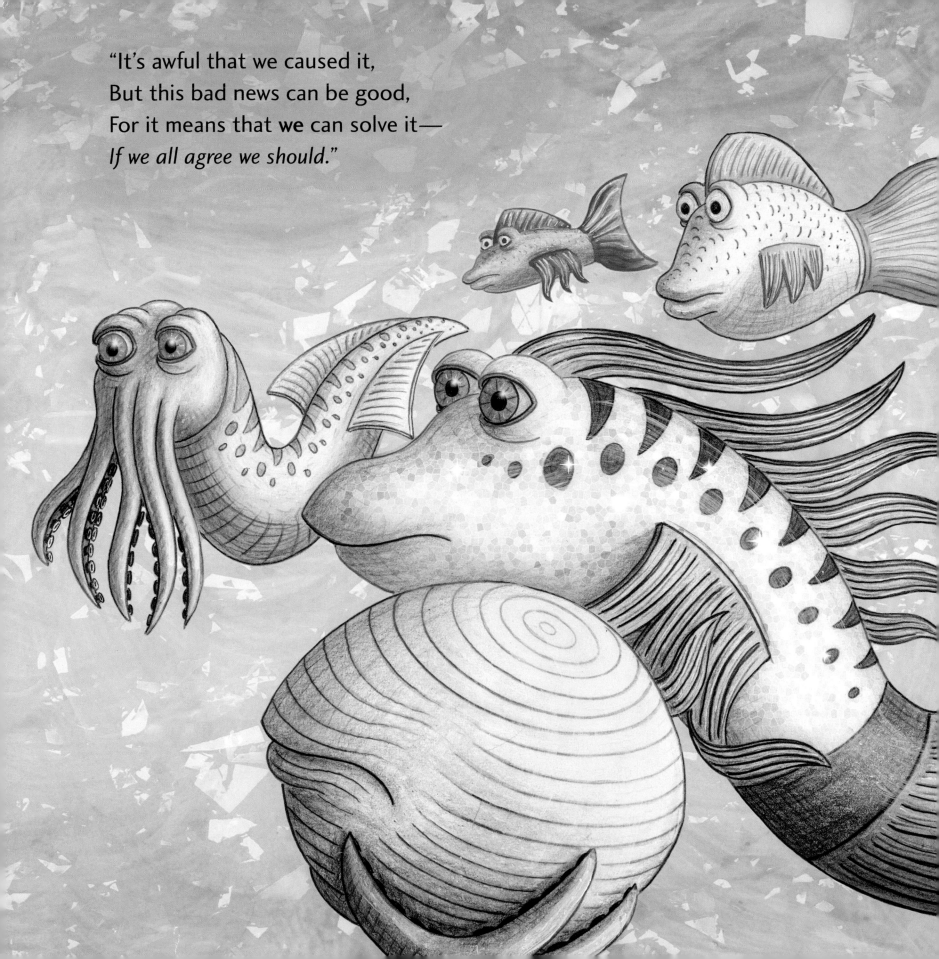

"It's awful that we caused it,
But this bad news can be good,
For it means that **we** can solve it—
If we all agree we should."

Silence filled the ocean.
Their future was at stake.
It was a moment of decision.
But which one would they make?

A big . . .
BIG . . .
"YES!!"

"We can do it!" they exclaimed.
"Positively! Yes and yup!"
So they all pitched in together
And they cleaned the ocean up.

They gathered up the garbage
With the help of everyone.

They worked hard to fix and remedy
The damage that they'd done.

Then they talked about new habits:
How to travel with less trace
And reduce their use of plastic
And put trash into its right place.

"Problems have solutions,
So we learn what we can do.
Together, we're the answer . . .

"Would you like to join us, too?"

**A note from the creators of
the Pout-Pout Fish series:**

Mr. Fish and his friends are counting on **you**! Even if you don't live anywhere near a beach, there are many things you can do to help clean up and protect the ocean.

Learn more. Your parents, teachers, and librarians can help you learn more about risks to our oceans. Some questions to ask include: What are the causes of ocean damage? Which ocean creatures are affected? How do changes in our oceans impact other parts of our planet?

Take action. Make choices based on what you learn. Can you use fewer packaged products and plastic containers? Can you participate in a trash cleanup? Can you carpool, or ride your bike instead of being in a car? In what other ways can you make a difference?

Grow the change. Tell others about what you learn and about the changes you're making. Knowledge is powerful, and good choices are contagious. Scale up the impact of what you're doing by sharing it with family, friends, neighbors, and community leaders.

Together, we're the answer! Thank you for joining us.